# Brady Brady
## and the Cranky Kicker

*Written by* Mary Shaw

*Illustrated by* Chuck Temple

PUBLISHED BY
BRADY BRADY INC.

Published in Canada in 2006 by

Brady Brady Inc.
P.O. Box 367
Waterloo, Ontario
Canada
N2J 4A4

**Library and Archives Canada Cataloguing in Publication**

Shaw, Mary, 1965 -
Brady Brady and the cranky kicker / written by Mary Shaw; illustrated by Chuck Temple
For children aged 4-8

ISBN-10   1-897169-08-6
ISBN-13   9781897169087


I. Temple, Chuck, 1962- II. Title.

PS8587.H3473B7323 2006          jC813'.6          C2006-904006-

Brady and his friends just want to kick their football and have a bit of fun. But everything they do
upsets old Mr. Luddy. He's the crankiest, meanest neighbor ever – and all for no good reason.
But wait. Maybe there is a reason, after all.

**Printed and bound in Canada**

*Keep adding to your Brady Brady book collection! Other titles include* **Brady Brady and the:**

- **Great Rink**
- **Runaway Goalie**
- **Twirlin' Torpedo**
- **Singing Tree**
- **Super Skater**
- **Big Mistake**
- **Great Exchange**
- **Most Important Game**
- **MVP**
- **Puck on the Pond**

*For Ali.*
*Thanks for the occasional "kick."*
*Your dedication and enthusiasm has meant so much*
Mary and Chuck

It was spring. Time to put away the hockey skates and get out the football. Brady was looking forward to a game with his friends – until he found his ball, flattened, the way he had left it at the end of last season.

Old Mr. Luddy had let the air out of it before giving it back, just because it had gone into his garden . . . again.

Brady headed outside to where his dad was working in the yard.

"Dad, my friends and I are going to play football. Can you fix it?"

Brady's dad found the pump.

"Brady Brady," he said, "please be careful. I don't want Mr. Luddy getting upset again this year."

"We didn't upset him on purpose.  Mr. Luddy is always cranky. Why do you think he is, Dad?"

"He and football don't mix, I guess. But he's a good neighbor. Try to keep the football out of his garden, okay?"
Brady promised, but he still thought Mr. Luddy was mean.

The kids were waiting on the empty lot when Brady arrived.

He was nervous as he set the ball down and lined up for the first big kick of the year. Brady had to keep the ball from going too far to the right – and into Mr. Luddy's yard.

Brady took a run,
wound up, and missed
the ball altogether.
He fell flat on his back.
His friends burst out
laughing.

"Oops! I guess I shouldn't worry so much
about where the ball is going."

**"What's with all the racket out here!"**

The kids jumped. It was Mr. Luddy.
His face was red and he was very upset.

"Sorry, Mr. Luddy," Brady replied
with a wave. "We'll try to
keep it down."

Mr. Luddy scowled and walked away.

"Whatever we do," said Brady,
"we better not kick the ball to the *right*!"

It was Kev's turn to kick.

As usual, he was talking too much when he hoofed the ball. It bounced along the ground, end over end, through the hedge, not stopping until it was in the middle of Mr. Luddy's vegetable patch.

The kids were terrified.

They played a game of Rock, Paper, Scissors
to see who would retrieve the football.

Brady got stuck with the job.

As Brady reached down
to pick up his football,
a huge foot stomped on it.

"You kids are testing my patience," grumbled Mr. Luddy. "Next time, you won't get your football back!"

With that he kicked the ball *waaay* to the far end of the empty lot.

Kev retrieved the football and then joined his friends in a group huddle.

"We have to be more careful," Brady said.

"That's for sure! Mr. Luddy was furious," added Tes.

"Yeah, but did you see how far he kicked the ball?" asked Kev.

Tes was up next. Chester did a few calculations and helped her line up the kick.

Tes leapt into the air, twirled in a circle, landed, and booted the ball with all her might.

High and straight, it was the perfect kick. That is, until . . . a gust of wind blew it off course – to the *right*!

The ball landed with a thud up against
Mr. Luddy's basement window.

"Uh-oh," said Chester.
His teeth began to chatter.

"What do we do now?" asked Tes.

"This time," Brady whispered,
"we all go and get it."

They stepped around the hedge
and tiptoed toward the
back of the house.

Brady could hear his heart thumping as he bent to pick up his football. As he grabbed it, something shiny caught his eye.

"Cool!" said Brady. The basement was filled with trophies and football pictures. In one corner was the biggest trophy he had ever seen.

"*HEY!*" What are you kids doing over there?" Mr. Luddy yelled, coming up behind them.

Clutching his ball, Brady stood up to face his neighbor.

But then, something in the old man's face changed, and Brady wasn't afraid anymore.

"Mr. Luddy," he said, "did you win that big trophy down there? Dad said you and football don't mix, but I think you must love the game as much as we do."

Without a word, Mr. Luddy turned and walked away.

The kids didn't feel like playing anymore, especially since they couldn't get past the opening kick.

They were sitting in the field when Brady spotted his neighbor carrying the huge trophy and a photo album under his arm.

Mr. Luddy set the trophy down and puffed out his chest.

"This trophy is The Bronze Boot," he said. "I won it for being the best place kicker in my league."

Mr. Luddy opened the album and showed them the pictures of himself when he was a young football hero. He told the kids his nickname had been Bull's Eye. Suddenly Mr. Luddy seemed sad.

He bent to gather up his things and knocked over the trophy. Brady picked it up to see if it was okay.

"Don't worry, Brady," said Mr. Luddy. "This trophy is nothing but bad luck, anyway."

"Bad luck!" Brady gasped. "How could that be?"

"After I won The Bronze Boot, our team went to the championship game. We were losing by two points and I was sent in to kick the winning field goal. The fans chanted my name. *'Bull's Eye! Bull's Eye! Bull's Eye!'* It was a sure thing . . . or so I thought." Mr. Luddy closed his eyes. "Like always, I kicked it straight and far. It was the *perfect* kick."

"But just then, a big gust of wind blew it off course. It went to the *right* of the goalpost. I had lost the game."

Mr. Luddy opened his eyes. "After that, I never played football again."

"Mr. Luddy!" cried Brady. "Would you like to play now? You're the best football player we've ever met. You could teach us how to play football for real!"

The kids all nodded in agreement.

"I'll teach you on one condition," said Mr. Luddy with a wink. "We spend some time on kicking first. That needs a lot of work, especially if my garden is going to survive!"

"Deal!" Brady replied, shaking his neighbor's hand.

Mr. Luddy joined the kids in a huddle.
They yelled their team cheer at the top of their lungs.

*"We've got the power,*
*We've got the might,*
*Kick the football left . . .*
*When the wind is blowing right!"*